D0997161

Everyone...

Christopher Silas Neal

WALKER BOOKS
AND SUBSIDIARIES

Sometimes ...

the day never seems to end.

You might be happy

one moment

and sad the next.

Or frustrated,

frazzled,

fed up,

bonkers,

batty,

bananas...

Ahhhhhh!

But no one seems to listen.

Sometimes, you just need to cry,
and that's OK.

When you cry, you are not alone.

When you laugh ...

happiness
grows.

And when you sing ...

everyone listens.

Everyone sings,

everyone laughs,

everyone cries every now and then.

Everyone has feelings, and that's OK.

Because everyone shares them...

Everyone.

For Jasper Silas Neal

First published 2016 by Walker Books Ltd
87 Vauxhall Walk, London SE11 5HJ

2 4 6 8 10 9 7 5 3 1

This book has been typeset in Century Schoolbook

Printed in China

British Library Cataloguing in Publication Data:
a catalogue record for this book is available
from the British Library

ISBN 978-1-4063-6842-0

www.walker.co.uk

FSC
www.fsc.org

MIX
Paper from
responsible sources
FSC® C008047